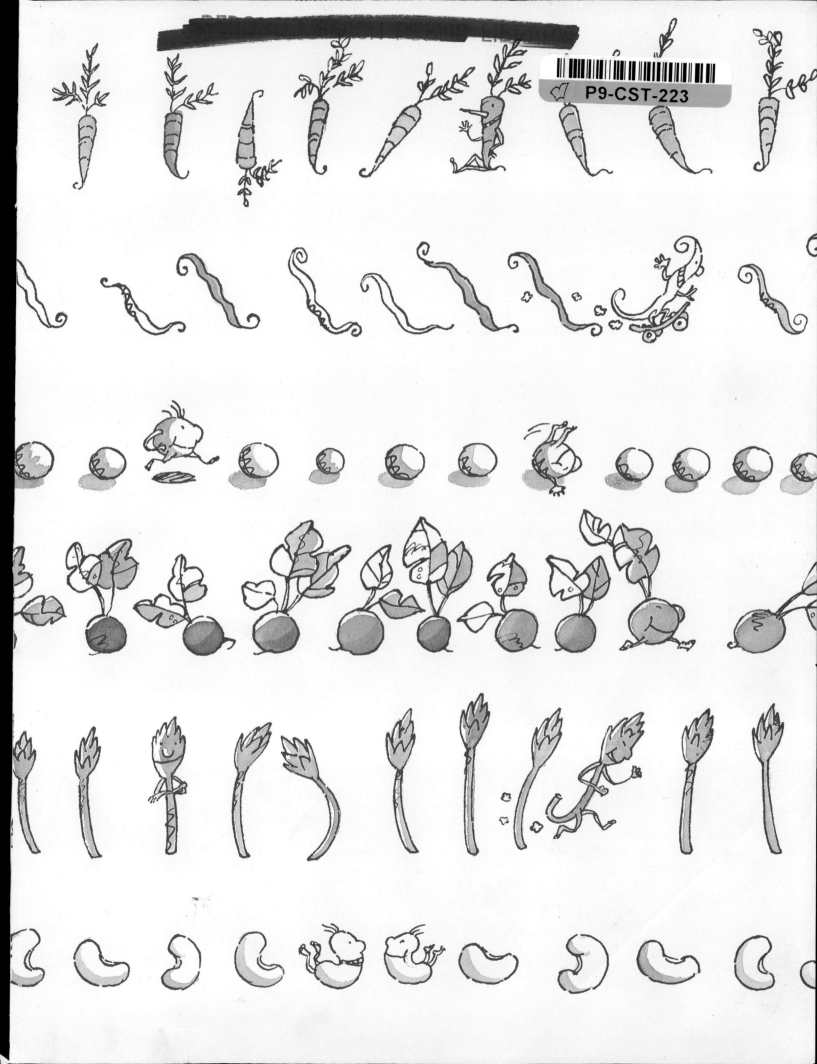

When Vegetables Go Bad!

WHEN VEGETABLES GO Bad!

Written by
DON GILLMOR

Illustrations by
MARIE-LOUISE GAY

FIREFLY BOOKS

For Andrew – *D.G.*
For Lucille – *M.-L. G.*

A FIREFLY BOOK

Copyright © 1994, 1998 text by Don Gillmor
Copyright © 1994 illustrations by Marie-Louise Gay

Cataloging in Publication

Gillmor, Don
    When vegetables go bad!

ISBN 1-55209-192-9 (bound) ISBN 1-55209-261-5 (pbk.)

I. Gay, Marie-Louise. II. Title.

PS8563.I59W5 1998   jC813'.54   C98-930891-X
PZ7.G54Wh 1998

Design by Avril Orloff

Published in the United States in 1998
by Firefly Books (U.S.) Inc.
P.O. Box 1338, Ellicott Station
Buffalo, New York, USA
14205

Printed and bound in Canada

he trouble
with Ivy was,
she wouldn't eat
her vegetables.

"Eat your vegetables," Ivy's mother said, "or you won't grow up to be big and strong."

Ivy stared at the blue flowers that were painted on her plate. She began to count them.

"Do you want them to go bad?" her mother said. "Do you?"

"Yes," Ivy said.

"Well, you are going to sit here until you finish those vegetables, young lady," her mother said, "if it takes all night."

Ivy stared at the vegetables. They were green and yellow and cold and damp. She would rather eat bugs. She stared at them for two hours and they got greener and yellower and colder and damper.

Ivy closed her eyes. She hoped that when she opened them, her vegetables would be gone. She opened her eyes and they were still there, though she thought they had moved. When her mother wasn't looking, she put all her vegetables in her napkin and stuffed it into her pocket.

"Finished," she said to her mother.

"There," she said, "That wasn't so bad now, was it."

"No."

Whern she went to bed, Ivy hung her pants over the chair. The vegetables were still in her pocket. She turned out the light and went to sleep.

Inside her pants pocket, a funny thing happened to the vegetables. They went bad. They began to sing:

In your pants

we all turned rotten.

All the green things

you've forgotten.

We've gone bad

and we'll get worse.

We'll follow you

just like a curse.

Ivy woke up and saw a turnip in the middle of her bedroom. It was almost as big as she was.

"I am a turnip," the turnip cried.

"I taste so good," the turnip lied.

There was a carrot leaning against the dresser, cleaning his teeth with a knife. A group of green beans was filling her shoes with rocks. In her closet, a stalk of broccoli was trying on her clothes and stretching her sweater. It was true. They *had* gone bad.

"Vegetables!" Ivy yelled. She sat up and looked around her room, her eyes adjusting to the dark. They had mushy faces and beady eyes. The carrot was green. The peas weren't. They sang:

We've been sitting
much too long.
You won't grow up
big and strong.

Inside her bedroom was every vegetable Ivy hadn't eaten. There was the lettuce from yesterday's lunch and the turnips she had put on her brother's plate at Thanksgiving. There was an army of peas, a herd of cauliflower, a forest of broccoli. A group of asparagus spears waved from the corner of the room.

I don't remember *them*, Ivy thought.

"We're the vegetables you wouldn't even *try*," they said. "You just *knew* you didn't like us."

"I like you now," Ivy said weakly. Their heads almost touched the ceiling.

"And what about us," the peas chorused. They were the size of basketballs. "Too mushy, too small, too *round*, you said."

The vegetables moved towards her, crowding Ivy's bed. The turnip was now bigger than her mother.

"You called me 'Nature's Great Mistake,'" the turnip said. He was bending over, his long finger touching Ivy's nose. "You said I was too *orange*."

"We were too *cold*," the beans said.

"I was too *warm*," the lettuce said.

"Too yellow!"

"Too green!"

"Too old!"

"Too mean!"

"Too ugly and damp
Too shrivelled and brown
Too mushy and small
Too stupid and round
Too much, too little
No room on your plate
You're sick, you're full,
You're trying to lose weight
They're never in season
They give me the willies
The beans are boring
The salad is silly."

Ivy lay on her bed, her eyes open in the dark. She could see her pants hanging over the chair. She thought about the napkin full of vegetables in the pocket and knew she had to do something about it. She couldn't leave them there. She got out of bed and walked slowly toward her pants. She stood for a moment before reaching inside the pocket.

It was empty. There was a crumpled napkin on the floor and out in the hall she thought she heard singing,

"Oh, we've gone bad,
        and we'll get worse ...."